*To Tannie —
The Perfect Neighbor*

The Alabaster Plant

Shannon L. Sanford

Copyright © 2003 by Shannon L. Sanford

ISBN 0-7414-1539-9

Published by:
INFIИITY
PUBLISHING.COM
519 West Lancaster Avenue
Haverford, PA 19041-1413
Info@buybooksontheweb.com
www.buybooksontheweb.com
Toll-free (877) BUY BOOK
Local Phone (610) 520-2500
Fax (610) 519-0261

Printed in the United States of America

Printed on Recycled Paper

Published October 2003

TABLE OF CONTENTS

PART I
ITEMS OR THINGS

Bust 2

Fan 3

Piano 4

Dandelion 6

Keys 7

Do Not Trespass 8

Honey 9

Chair 10

Small Flower 11

The Remainder of the Day (Part I Summary) 12

PART II
DESCRIPTIONS AND METAPHORS

Old Tom 16

London Nights 17

Historical Home 18

14th Street 19

The Opera 20

The Quiet Furious Blizzard 22

Imperfect Color . . . . : 24

Regret 25

Destiny or Will 26

Nightmare 27

Family Heirloom 28

Family Heirloom (Second Rendition) 29

Dead Branch 30

Manta Rays 31

Final Judgment 32

Aged Wine 33

Nine Children 34

Naughty Books 38
Roots 39
Small Citrine 40
Victory 41
Halls of Tall 42
I Did Notice 43
Dusky Duck 45
Victorious (Part II Summary) 46

PART III
CHARACTERS

Floorboards to Bells 50
The Novice Wine Taster 52
Night Dog 53
Walking Right Over My Grave 54
Cauldron Awaits 56
Vertical Kings 57
Lonely Rat 58
Black and White Captures 59
Flight Attendant 60
Insanity the Scavenger 61
Mourning Imagination 63
Irish Warriors 64
Walking Staff 65
Subway Train: The Shoes of Passing People 66
Once the Tempest Doth Run Out (Part III Summary) 67

PART IV
INJUSTICES

Never You'll Know 72
Discrimination 74
Many Hours 75

Youthful Life 76

Before 78

Injustice Grand Scale (Part IV Summary) 79

PART V
LAND AND LEADERSHIP

Long Last This Lass the Ruler 84

Yellowstone 86

Well-Decorated General 87

Column 89

Leadership 90

Perilous Vault (Part V Summary) 91

PART VI
TALES AND SHORT STORIES

Haunted Forest 96

Big Foot Bearing Fruit 97

Halls of My Home 99

Basement Shroud 102

Question the Lunar Walk 104

The Alabaster Plant 105

Fact or Fiction (Part VI Summary) 119

PART VII
PHILOSOPHY AND TIME

The Republic 122

Under the Board 123

The Academy 124

The Vegetarian 126

Routine 127

Wisdom 128

Merry-Go-Round 129

The Gift of Sanguine 132

Splinters 133

We Too Shall Be Forgotten 134

First Lesson on Greed 136

The Glastonbury House 137

Misery Unchecked 138

(Untitled) 139

Consideration of Clock 140

The Bribe 141

Insipid Hourglass 142

Exulted Ends: I Walk to Them 143

Simultaneous 145

Serendipity (Parts I - VII Summary) 147

This book is dedicated to my loving husband, Douglas, who spent endless hours over the years inspiring and critiquing poems of *The Alabaster Plant*.

For which I am eternally grateful.

Important Note From the Author

The first time you read ***The Alabaster Plant***, it is crucial that it be read from beginning to end and not in a haphazard order. The poems build upon themselves and are divided into seven parts progressing from simple to complex insights. There is a summary poem for each particular part. However, the last summary poem of the seventh part is a culmination of themes and imagery from the entire book.

If this book is not read in chronological order the first time, the overall comprehension and/or impact may be lost.

The Alabaster Plant was completed in its entirety with an original copyright date of June 2001. The new copyright date of April 2003 reflects the date of actual publication.

PART I

ITEMS OR THINGS

Bust

Transform hairs of life and wrinkles
Which move in motion of spirit
Into clay that solidifies like rock lava on a stump
Hard to cold the forms firmed

Stands now as emblem of history
A noble one well known
Adorns the rooms of many a wealthy home
My head alone

Fan

Fan to mix the molecules
Shifting laughter to far off corners
Not the giggle's intended goal
Words formed
Gasped out of mouth
To wild winds of small technology that swaggers speech
Fast they ebb to echoes
From the swivel of blades

Piano

I, over in corners, in the din
Beneath the stage front, a pit
My pitch not played, futile neglected years
No fingers for keys and keys
Strings brittle with little use
The blacks, the whites, some cracked
       maddening

Deserted in the murky dust
Settling in layers down
From coffered ceilings of old opera house
Wherein I used to be the star player
Even Brahms plundered quick scales
       at one time

Now in the adumbrate forgotten
Laughable memento
Of languid days hurdling voices to mezzanines
Throwing visages, all gaunt white paint
Then full red lips spread wide, the ample woman
Pelts out charmed, eerie voice soprano
Surpassing the torrent roar
       of the piano

I, deathly staked, left in corners designate
       to disintegrate
Slowly over the dawn of new band's play
Yesteryears echo round the empty chambers
I can hear faintly
       if I were to hear it
All ladies clad in gowns and gold so near it
Fading to the turrets

Curtain drawn down
Audience withdraws applause
Ladies' butterfly fans close

Whip shut
White gloves exit to the left
Deport to the right
Disparaging night

When upon one eve
They did banish my euphony forever
Replaced with faultless black sleek grand
Made as kindred
            only no benefit of mine

Outdated and told to the back
Sitting here, unusable hutch
Hated loss of climaxing pitches
            that I minored and majored

Please leave eloquently
            if you'll not play me

Dandelion

Come the last hour
The token yellow lion
Later till August becomes white plumes
With hope
Swishing the white lights feathered
To the moon

A wish

Keys

In old day doors they did not enter for folly
        to take that which was not theirs
Yet today as we look upon our doors
        worry overtakes the times before
Born the rigid lines of key clasps to distinguish the doors

To keep the stranger out once welcomed
        or the child within from straying
All we need today is this grooved coin to determine
        entrance or denial

As danger rounds around the world of robbery or toke
We must have these keys to lock us
        from stray and jailbird folk

Do Not Trespass

Barbary wire
That pulls and cuts and tears

Not over
Not under
Not through

What to do with the barbwire
You can't get through
Barbaric blasted wire

Damn, here come the dogs!
Hear my ire!

Honey

Length that licks the bud of upward sprout
Pink against green
So vivid beauties

Bumble of yellow black slips to petal
Then inside for nectar of the day

Transport honey bounced on back
Released to support the nest
Swarming in hive of home

The cycles

Chair

Chair of dark mahogany wood and yellow gold seat
Your color still outshines me
Years of past to dine upon thee

Yet with cruel specter I did spectate
Found none of which to match your kind
Made with seat or wood as fine

As though to speak like predecessor
To sit upon the cushion lofty
Harnessed by history

Not to rant and rave and so on
Just to say,
     "Old chair of gold cushion
      I sat you many years beneath me
      Still you seem more than me
      Even many holidays
      Is it your antiquity that impacts?"

On I go to grandmother's home
Feels as though my own
Not what I want true

But somehow it is just so
On golden mahogany
Remembering

Small Flower

My days seem as a bed of vines
    that twist upon each other
Even when I think them straight
    in baths of buoyant colored bouquets
Though the vines do deeply twist
    I roll amongst them
In wonderment of one small flower

Taking in fragrances of my life
How fragrant its splendor dispels
Only the petals foretell the fairytale
    that is my life
Immersed in one small flower

When winter befalls my garden
    flowers wilt as vines freeze
And I wait longingly beside their roots till spring
    where again I may see the story
In the hottest of noon hours
    amongst the vines swimming to the petal
Of one small flower

The Remainder of the Day

Blowing winds wildly around my living room parlor
This heat needs blades to swivel till cool
Summers noon hour is upon us
Entered with trusty key, inside for relief
Hottest day expelled me from the garden
Allowing me to work no more
No more
        for the remainder of the day

How the bees have nourished my garden to full earthy bloom
Buoyant bouquets dispelled round me
And my favorite tulip that seems to outlast the last seed
I rolled amongst its vines today
Before the pestering sun took me away
Away
        for the remainder of the day

I am cooling slightly now, with easy chills
Breezy, heady and reflective
Upon this chair
Oh, how grandma did relish her golds and darks
Whereupon, I sit and brood
        for the remainder of the day

Eyes tiredly roll to his fine skull
Outlines in dark stealthy etchings
To wear dignity upon his brow
Yes, grandfather sits now as bust upon my hutch
Revered by all and to all well known
Honored to have his hardened presence slated upon my home
I think of him alone
        for the remainder of the day

He reached far into earth for tumult and success
While all I shall have is a flowering garden
With buds that burst and swell with bees returning seasonal
The last I hear is key fallen to clank the floor
Ah, the heat is faded
As I begin to nap in dreams upon the vines
Of one small flower where I slumber in my nesting mind
        for the remainder of the day

PART II

DESCRIPTIONS AND METAPHORS

Old Tom

Pick if you please
From the bounteous fields
Many hands to the earth for the ripe

A simple man
The giver of life
Old man overalls
Kneel down to test soil
For richest production
So particular the fruit, the tomato
Growers manhandle the acreage
Into a blooming tower, the sower
Forsaken all his days into one tiny pear
Apples in bundles cut
Grapes into peach sizes
Trees of fruit surround the plentiful growing vegetables
The perfect oasis for cultivating, many seasons

Suddenly, old Tom yells out
A stricken frenzy from afar
Equipment gone ajar
And taken his arm

Alarmed, the fruit dropped to soil
Farmer off to the trauma that toils
Little importance this pear that fell
Compared to plight

A minor matter it seems
For the pear upon the floor
The spoiler of dreams

London Nights

Upward steps of doldrums, fluorescent bulbs and filthy walls
Garnished with janitor buckets and brooms
Jingling key through rusted rooftop lock
Wrangling till just the right upward stroke

Door frees and opens

Fog stains skies as doves nest on London rooftops
Grateful recovery of keys weeks hence lost
Night air awakens soul to thought
Unlock sullen turmoil upon rooftop glaze

Myself alone and unaccustomed

Soothing elements compel
Shingles many shapes and pitch heights varied
Lonely scoundrel left to remember

Chimney palpates and smokes

Mingling aroma of night, mistiness, firewood and cement
Heave thick moisture beads upon my face
Leaning against faithful wall viewing all of quiet London
Peaceful place to light lanterns scattered

Church bells pendulum and chime

Struck till crescendos transcend clock tower
Ears ring with slashing tongues that reached no meaning
Might peace burst forth in flight through dawn's first light

Doves fly and flourish

Historical Home

White
Like cracked pearls clasping an elderly throat

Aged
As fading scents of peach and apple pies

> Baked in hearth of old home
> In floors that creak and walls sliced by time
>> where reflected

> His chair in front of flames
> Yellowed wallpaper pulls down from his smoke
>> many ashes

She gazes through panes surrounded by cracked white pearls of paint
The frames of aging windows of this house

14th Street

There we live on 14th Street
Near the corner store
Where walks the feet
A beggar here or there
A wealthy not fare
Never into the groves of despair

Pity for the poor not a thought
For their eyes
Where I reside
On the eastern side
The favorite cop beat
A misery street

The Opera

High pitched

The bellows of art gathered in years
To decades rolling and roaring
The scent of old lady flowers
Expelled from their breath
Outward gasp the fairytale epic and operatic
Stroke the keyboards
Thrash the gong
Thronging

The trilogies

Undoubted singers forever displayed
Amongst the human maze
Effortless hearts rise and sing the pit to pitches
Unsung
Unheard
The sinewy word
Encapsulation of the title and conflict

Wherein the story breeds anew

Impregnating the very instances of life
Invoked upon the pages
Upon the chords
The voice soars
Over balconies tiered
Around again and back up the towers of the town
That ring at midnight

This eve the opera did sing

And hold the city still
Upon its place
Low the baritone to moan around a thousand dwellings

Frozen in glass of voices holding storefronts high in octaves
Trapped in splendor
Upon the stained glass
Rendered

Ever out of love and thus equate the man

Upon his syllable sung
And breath await
To counter all incontinence
Inside the sound
The vibe
We eternally stride
Captured in one opera hour

Ringing through the night

The Quiet Furious Blizzard

Softly Monday's dawn swathes lawns, tiny shimmers
Slowly open eyes and rest awhile longer
As melons pre-cut await the morning meal, so little effort
Smelling bacon smoked, coffee wafting

Cranking comfort from roasted beans
To soothe and fully awaken
Morning scents
Roused into thoughts of the day ahead

To the garden, to the store and lastly, the bank
Before heaviest snow sets in at blizzard lengths
When all is peace and balmy
The calm before the discord

Frenzied storm soon to propel in furious forms
Multitudes of flakes will shower as feathers to earth's floor
Pushed hard and fast, downward dusting
Sinewy whites softly repel millions down in spells

Flatten city curbs to smooth level whites upon whites
Until the urban sprawl as country plains and hills
From wind drifts swept up against the pillars
And builds upon walls until the mortar sets to chill

And climb them up till clouds
Moisten windowpane
Wiping circles, peeking out
The world seems as one white entity
Gently, from ground flakes to lofty clouds

That pile upon the walls
All locked inside of doors
No school nor labor allowed
Demanded by the storm

Restful down into blankets and beds
Dreaming, winter cherubs whispering lullabies
On shoulders heavily rest, half dozing
Above the urban sprawl, the winter birds call
Quietly

Imperfect Color

As I stare at the wall that resides beside impressive painting
Something is amiss
For greatest waxen colors flicker from the canvas
          and darkest detailed frame surrounds her skin

Lady of red hair
Encircled in beautiful pale pinks and jovial green flowers
Pales the wall of imperfect color
Unsuitable homely wall!
How dare you show your face near hers
I feel the need to strike your blandness with a brush
Brutishly with colors to match this flame of frame

Yet unacceptable for me, unskilled, even to tarnish your bland surface
Though you are less than her, I am less than you
So it seems, most boring wall, you must be left in the vicinity of greatness
          with your most imperfect color

Regret

Dragon enters my commune
Never allowing sleep

Fire to breathe memoirs forward in flames
Red orange to unstill these silent nights to savagery

Winged reptile to escape my venom
Harm has hardened the blows of wounds

Dares to leave before I can revenge him in my cave
Unable to silence words that left me slain

With own sword did not strike back
Taunted ceaselessly with my past

As no revenge I can regain

Destiny or Will

Fangs snarl neck to tear tiny beast to blood
Stronger feet of sure swift locomotive legs
Rapidly outrun and capture
Nightly feast wrapped in hulking paws
Dried red splashing stains
      onto hunter from the prey

Truth discovered in such displays
Do we whimper and whine
Slump our shoulders to defeat
Until discarded as weakness
Or smell the opportunity so rarely dealt and leap upon it

Some would rather bloody their fangs in the flesh of another
      and take life in their own hands
      than to be weak and defeated
Letting life itself take them out of living

So are we the privy hunter sculpting destiny to our will
      or the tiny prey where life lives us
      and wrangles us till still

Nightmare

This frenzied pace
       of pushing leaves faster down than rain

This whipping tarantula
       from the downspout to the hedges
Crawling loud clicks across my windowpane

This night
The fragile endeavor of a dream
That peeks through and takes no lessons
And brings lightning brighter than the sun
That strikes without thunder
       as the elm scratches the pane near my bed
For hours it seems
       until all is spent

And then
This blessing
       of arachnophobia eyes
       staring into mine
From my chest a shallow breath
Bitten on the breast
Until all is dead

And in the dawn
It is forgotten

Family Heirloom

Adorning amulets
Scribbling in soot on roof
Scroll through confusing dialect
Unknown
Bastardly acts
Dexterity lasts forever

Ruby red stone set in bronze
Bleak to doves above
Below rooms leading nowhere
Unfound
Commiserate
Ever proud was he

Engraved words endeared
Reflective sun shards illuminate metals
Mazes exit to freedom
Then recognized
Life commemorates
The righteous prevail

Past thorns

Family Heirloom

(Second Rendition)

Adorning amulets
Ruby red stone set in bronze
Engraved words endeared

Scribbling in soot on roof
Bleak to doves above
Reflective sun shards illuminate metals

Scroll through confusing dialect
Below rooms leading nowhere
Mazes exit to freedom

Unknown, unfound
Then recognized

Bastardly acts commiserate
Life commemorates

Dexterity lasts forever
Ever proud was he
The righteous prevail

Tranquility today

Dead Branch

Dripping sap from old Acer trees
Does not forsake this one branch upon its lushness
To shut out and let it whither
While others burst forth with greenery

Only the strongest survive

Manta Rays

Manta rays rise
As lily pads I walk upon
The odd pond
To the shores
Imbedded with golden beams
The fantasy

Play out the words
Murmuring mystical woods
Where swans try to dive under the golden fawns
Near pansies blue
Ducks descend near
Sparkling tides shimmering in the midday sun
Frogs happy helpings of croaks
Flittering fairies I cannot see
Swim next to me
When I am doused in the pond
Not strolling atop the stinging lilies

Instead strewn with creatures in their beds
With which I'm wed
One with nature
The speller of all trivial trials
And mine none the less
As I swim and sift on golden waters
In gleams of a request
From fairies enchanted

Final Judgment

Assailing sin from certain masses
Creature themselves into warlike fashions
To fight and clash

While others give ungreedy - getting none
Emerge to hold fellow man till luminous in love
To compassion and unearth

Rapt the air that bounces upon itself
Mingling love and hate forms
As they transcend to sudden blue gone
Into weightlessness - traverse they on

To upward kingdom - mobile domes
Where seraphs await to grasp both masses
And fetch them to our divinity

Until the judgment final

Aged Wine

Green bottle bearing vast blue labels
Fermentation of sweetest crushed grapes
Hand picked from vines that grew inside a forest
Where deeply sleeping man awakened
Marveling at the world and one like him
Yet fashioned with the curves of creation

Hence from tiny cells of trees and seas came beasts
From algae to animals
From leaves to clothes
From hunting to vocation
From meager shelters to protruding structures
From foot to vehicles
Many vessels
Convenience by a thousand fold
Sending us from village to town
Into sprawling cities
Sequestered by countries
Hastened for the advance
Reeling speeds surpassing
Usurping all tides into one futile race
As though to exploit the axis ever quicker
For the purpose

Until a craving for wet woodlands
Wherein a thousand vintages of life
Ripen on the vine
Until the palm picks it
Frontal lobes escorted by the primitive
Seduced by origins

Nine Children

Contemplative and authoritative
Look up the blue as far as you can
See beyond the simple human head
Further than the reaches of downy clouds
Up through the stratosphere
Wholly round and queer
To the eight ineptitude spheres
Where exists no life but gas, rock, and ice

The first relative to Einstein
Mercury positioned as a smaller sun dance
But cooler than the further one
Too close to the fire spreading and plotting
To be hotter by the hour
Spattering and sputtering the lava compared
To the speeding Hermes of mc^2

The second babe was a she
A beautiful V
A Venetian Venus
Wrapped with the sexy name used on Earth
As though Earth must be her man
Hotter than the speeding Hermes
A fire pistol Aphrodite
Unruly winds of gasses
Though many hues shade her lava grasses
Untamed and wild Venus to the ramparts

The third of parts
Most intelligible
And eligible for life
Named for the English Germanic
The Earth I sit and toil each day
Now staring through its blues
The single moon and a core hotter than the sun
From layered mantles to regions and crusts

Laying down upon the greens that thwart
The atmosphere to a living thing
Ah, most resonant of all
Most powerful in this order is a middleman
Come lay beside its borders

The fourth from lots
Mars of red rock
Everywhere the same sienna color of an Ares god
A grand Olympus Mons
Exposing extra-terrestrial forms
Once tectonics and greenhouse effect
A possible water flow - now gone

Next the fifth
The enormous orange and unattractive
Born as Jupiter
Four moons and convected gasses
Light banded zones and dark banded belts with a spot
Resembling a horned being
A veracious creature
A rotund bludgeoning beast
An awkward gaping Big Foot
As a one-eyed dragon bully of eight
Stupid and large, nothing visceral
Maybe many moons but none else
Accept the capacities of a pig
Apology to this boon buffoon-like thing
Let me please just pass around you
To the next light looming thing

Come Saturn to the sixth kin
As millions miles pass within
The rings that surround and suspend
Cassini division and ice water beds
Splendid shepards of twenty-one moons
Beckoning the swirling gasses to a glowing gray
White twirling with the pussy willows

Whispering in that exact shade
The mother of rings and moons and grays

Uranus, the seventh cold
Dark blue shades you as a Third George
Or the father of Cyclops and Titans
Tiny is your reign
Though rock and ice rings
Almost missed you
Like a dot unpretentious to any moons

Bit more dexterous, somehow brighter
Bluer and cooler, shinier and wider
Neptune named like many a nymph
Or great Poseidon from the farthest myths
Racing winds and shifting dark spots
A fairytale glow and fantastical aura
An amusement from afar
Lifeless but wondrous
A jolly sparkler
A fathomless star

The last, the least, and the leery
The farthest line of inquiries
Ends at the ninth
A Hades of coldest degrees
Hundreds thousands send to freeze
In perpetual dark of a controversial question
A planet of rock
Or an astral projection
The Antarctic child
A continent of cold
A chilly bone
The last one

Solar spree ends suddenly
Back around the universe
And through the abominable forces

So I may land again
On the earthly grass to greet and remember fondly
The tour of a billion years on an astral trolley
Through stellar denominations
Around cosmological foundations
And cleave to the dear floor beneath
For it is just the right ensuing seed

To sow our life

Naughty Books

Oh, naughty books of schoolyard hope
Never show us beyond the page
Taught us how to work for others
And not extend further

Cancel the exploration
What everyone seems to do
Why now have you trapped us

Oh, text fall to the floor
For you are causing us to miss beyond the page
Though none can exceed the book for intellect
To stretch for test
Grasp the far-fetched
But never can it teach one brilliant lesson

How to really live

Roots

Only notice the splendor of sprucing tree king
Never look beneath for roots of sovereignty
Ignore torturous labor to hold tree erect grand scale
Only the top is envied amongst small pin eyes

Oh, what we have endured
Insects ravage us to bare raw
Still we re-grow where we have been eaten
So redwood may stand
Tall amongst tall tree friends
And forget the foundation

Small Citrine

A glimpse of shimmer in oldest of wretched boxes
Passed from the eldest aunt to few children left
We pawed and prodded the pieces to a pilfering mess
Greedy to fetch the most beautiful of given jewels

I beheld one for which no one held interest
My interest it held

Long and rectangular
Golden gem and tarnished chain
Draping the neck most ornately a way

As the days of kingdoms
When experimentation of goodwill
          to charm the innocent maids
With lingering roses lost of vase
          laced in hair

Eyes of need fulfilled by men of wordy ways
In the contest of culture to win fair ladies' hearts
Even tragedies of many loves lost - only left is a tear
          from much ignored celebration
          of epoch romantic years

Small citrine
Infinitely cherished
Donned above my breast on most blessed day
This wedding
          October of autumn

Victory

Sweat and dried blood - old injuries
Athletes stare to goal post
Erected for all stadium spectators
As sweat beads form - the skill and drive to perform

Rush up and swing back to kick the past losses behind
And shoot
Thrust through leg
Pop hard and high
To the days since high school fields of guys
For fame to reach the skies

Field goal

Halls of Tall

Into wild tall humidity endless
Like a maze unbending to the ways that lead home

Huge jade heads topping bodies
So hefty wide
Roots sifting as larva burrowing forth between my toes
I walk on in hopes of home

Roots hold erect greatest redwood giants
Continue forth growing outward
Sweating, I grope on through garland beauties
Leaves reduced to tiny sizes

Halt
Behold largest of all hardiest trees
Redwood rather wilt than fall!
Cross atop its roots that give life to tree of tall
This tree amongst a maze of wooden halls

Scrambling

Will I get through
Will home hasten

I Did Notice

Water spawned with piranha
Some livestock they take
Tear whatever they may
Into nourishment of the day

Rimmed round the torrent
The most unseemly of groups
The buffalo, zebra, giraffe and cockatoo
And so many more
Lining opposite shores
Where borders menacing creatures
Without care for the horders
Slinking jauntily with muscles
Tight on tiger lions
Eyeing the many warily
Pawing their kill
Licking paws
Sleeping in weeds tall

Rampant insects
Loud buzzing
Flies swirl annoyingly shore to shore
Side to side
Scanty steps on fur and reptilians alike

Cockatoos dueling
Over some feign little fish
Crocodile eyeballs pursuing
Only above the water line
Creeping for the kill
Any warm-blooded thing
Jaws snap
Loud crack
And the struggle ensues
The fighting begins
And the piranha join in

To a massive splattering of the surge
Sprouting upwards
Splashing and thrashing accumulates
With speeds surpassing
Maximal velocities

Small-feathered birds fly up
Quick away
Grunting rhinoceros simply lays down to play
Many furs fly fast a few feet from the border
Escaping the fighting and venomous horders
Snakes slither delicately to water
Then land
Fangs pierce for a threat or eggs in the sand

When water stills from stir
Come back all the herds
The most unlikely a gathering
Of reptiles and fur

The furred and the feathered, the scaled and the large
The cacklers, the crowers, the growlers, the small
The insects, the pestilence, the python of venom
The rotund, the lithe-like, the scavenger, the venison
The simple, the privy, the conduit vulture
Sits most unusual a group round this commune of water

Set together in most oddly a fashion
I did notice
With laughter
Grief and compassion

Dusky Duck

Waves that lilt and fold on flattest shore
Break soft and stretch so vast
Sun glistens of gold a path atop the water
Boats beckon sounds from far and then near
Seemingly cracking the silence to speed

I watch the sun as it glides below the ridge
Leaving shadows on the timber beneath my feet
At last, a last inch of sun dissolves behind the range
In a sliver of sun's shadow something swims adrift
I stretch to toes and glimpse lonely feathered beast
Of pointed beak and web knot feet

So similar am I to this animal in the dusk
When hardest days deprave all needs
Shunned and left in darkness with none to hear my plea

Duck slowly swims downstream
Shifty, as though in search of kin
As I distance from my blooded ones

I swim on in search of familiarity before the sun sets and blinds the sight
Meandering in darkness with just these feathers seems to be my plight
No flight tonight for duck in dusk bathed in pale moonlight
Goodnight

Victorious

Victorious are those from whence we came
Born from grace down unto halls of forests
Culminating every living thing into our vintage glorious
Shed upon the land was a fulsome blood
And it grew into a man

Victorious world of seas and trade
Sparse economies to vast markets
The hand exchanging currencies
As passage through the world
Until tasted vintage aged

Victorious artists and artisans perfected their craft
Upon pages bleeding words expertly till souls drawn
Urging some to text trappings
Then freed with paint blown into relief on canvases
Many a vision designed on walls ensconced in spaces
Many places

Victorious stucco walls from shrines of brick
To erect historical home upon the hill where it now sits
Wherein he rests reflecting, blazing hearth
Smoke billows from fire shaping memories in white
Proud to raise children on old duck pond
She gazes through aging windows forever far and fond
Ducks flutter

Victorious elder woman considering the eras
From primates to modern lines
Gazing through the times
Through white cracked paint of aging window frame
Aware she had the best
Clutching old citrine
Resided on her chest
Ducks multiply

Victorious old man from his chair to her side
For one more stroll around the pond
Before the sun is gone
Into wind blowing gracefully
Across their aging face
Flawless moon soon to rise
One duck left in evening's tide

Balancing books on roots of trees
Reading passages near paintings
Emblazoned on the walls
Rearing youngsters in the studies
Following the world over
Changing round the tide
Now reflective old man and woman eyes
Leaving nothing to ponder and none undone
Victorious now to die

Feathers disappear
Sun shone and gone
Upon a life surrounded by this world around a pond
Their reminisces fond

And victorious

PART III

CHARACTERS

Floorboards to Bells

As carnival bells yell
Cotton candy sticks to fingers
Wiped on
Walls behind the sideshow
    demented memories dispel
    play out
    tears to tongue
No longer can hear so well
When the thump, thump, thump up the stairs
Of a father
Who hated me so obviously
    as he poured his raging whiskey breath across my talons
    and soaked his slapping grace against my face
    many days
And in the night
When I heard the floorboard creak
I knew it was he
Come to box my ears and posture them out with burning
    unsure was I
    of my crime
Only whiskey could foretell the rages
And why, oh why, he slapped by and by
Over and over till the thump of his foot to the slap of my ear
Rings now with the carnival bells that chime so near
    ears moan weak
    and clang head loud
Now the clown cackles
Dissonant melodies reel
As I fear he is near
With loud claps of whiskey upon deafening ears
So I dash to my castle
Abandoned church with dark vestibule
And play old piano fierce

To make sure I can hear I pound and I pierce
To degrees that blow my quiet ear to storm and then fury
I strike those cracked keys till blown and dust puffs up
And emasculates its every Latin tone upon the plow

I am Ludwig
Deafened to show of the sound
And the thunder of my past you hear
Which I cannot
Rings vast eternal 'pon these carnival grounds

The Novice Wine Taster

Grapes and seeds
Punched by a thorn
Dripped
To a deep raspberry bitter
A cranberry hint of subterfuge

Perhaps a swish of the goblet shall free it
The essence spinning

Little spots of cork sinking in the whirling center
A burning berry bush
A deep cinnamon gone bad

Red as velvet in winter
Or purple oil with blood drops

Up the flat syrupy concoction
Under the palate

Nothing like the aroma

Night Dog

Gray foul smelling beast
Only comes about at night
While others weary and fast asleep
Oh, night dog

When I saw your gray eyes
I realized there are dogs that only traipse the earth at night
Escape the ills that remain in your domain

If you only howl at the moon
When no one stirs and you're alone
You come around at night
And leave your troubles far behind at home
Oh, night dog

Walking Right Over My Grave

Resting today asleep in my grave
Skin used to cover bones that remain
Ashamed of past failures
Duties neglected
Materials purchased hoarded collected
Wears of fine jewels still crest round my knuckle
Large stranded pearls rest on my chest
Then comes circling a stranger
A pest
Walking right over my grave

Who is this person not to respect
Body and soul as it lays here to rest
To circle and saunter and not even wonder
Of the dignified life which now rests in slumber
To trample and kick the sod from my lid
And offer no solace or prayers for my bid
Thundering carelessly smashing me down
Forgetting the pressure that moves throughout ground
Who is walking over my grave

Must be a child
So uncaring and free as I used to be
Trampling and playing
Coloring my plaque
Dibbling and babbling
Tit for tat
Up to no good
Vandalizing peaceful gravesite
Only for games and frivolous plights
To giggle and gabble words of no sense
Pouncing on grave of many years hence
Someone is walking right over my grave

If adult it be
I'll bet it's lifelong foe
Just trying to get in those last licks and blows
Not caring for hell where surely she'll go
For rummaging my grave
Cruel trick or a joke
For stealing and wheeling and backhanded dealing
For error of my ways
She comes back to my grave
To serve one final kick
Running through quick
Without thought
Without sound
Churning the ground

Plowing and reeling without remorse or kind feeling
Dancing and dollop and prancing and wallop
Till I feel my bones shake
As they crack and they quake
Unearthing my grave
Unaware without care
Trembling coffin of horrid nightmare
I sit and I simmer and I curse the gods high!
Which is why my soul in this coffin resides

Stepping around a bit
Respecting my grave
Too much for the sinister and lazy
Or the juvenile crushing my fresh-cut lain daisies
Restless and angry and vengeful and crazy
Someone's walking right over my grave!

Cauldron Awaits

Craft of witch brewed to center hot
On holiday of 'Hallows Eve
Not only when they surround alters
To brew herbs with coercive words
Witches claim their craft
Spells cast

Cold now comes
October round the corner of colored leaves
Firewood splinters its scent upon the midnight air
As witches craft their brew
To remind you
Be wary

Vertical Kings

Pinnacle pointed
Broad base
Moon reflected on slanted verticals
Boulders shove the dome to point
Dragged stealthily on shoulders of thousands by ropes
Slaves driven to somewhat meaningless structure goal
For a king
Watching down on the many backs of bronze below

Built to the sun, skin sweats
Barefoot to hot sand, they drag
Passing camels, smelling foul
Boulders slowly, achingly

So today the picture may be shot
Expelled with quick flash bulb
Burning the image to transparencies
So modern men may reflect upon stoic structures
Angled high with hands
To greet the sky of a Pharaoh past
So him forever reflected in the sands
Upon which stands
Slanted vertical shrines of lands

Lonely Rat

There
In shadows of the darkest corridor
A comrade I caught a glimpse of
      or one of many faces lost from the past
Taunting me
      a soul to confide in aside from my own

Perhaps a mere reflection of the loneliness
For when the figure appears
      it is sooner gone
Till only shadows fill the murky hall
I remember the features
Mostly their eyes
      filled with the estrangement I caused

No matter what I thought I saw
      all that remains is empty space
And this craving
For something never possessed
Left to scavenge for hidden aged milk
      that longs and never finds
Due to internal flaws unredeemed

It is said, for a creature such as this, companions matter not
Then why the emptiness that leaves this scavenger so distraught

Black and White Captures

Shutter snaps and stills all time
Black and white

Peering above book to say, "Don't you get that close."

Half in darkness, half in light
The book, body, and eyes

Glancing from pages to repeat, "Not that close."

Knees drawn and quartered
Past wounds

Flight Attendant

Open layered
Bags aboard
Closed in aisle
Unharmonious colors
Seats straight
Blue and orange
      as others

Brightest red uniform
Stops to serve above her breast
Cart atop rollers
Talons of some eagle or such upon her chest
Catches the sun from my tiny circle sifter

Hands another drink
Full red-lipped smile
      vacant eyes

Insanity the Scavenger

Dementia of afflictions
Where psychosis rules the day
And no one speaks of divinity
So all are forsaken to white walls
And drugged till staggered
As the man is further removed
Amongst white spired walls padded thus
Straps to arms impeded
Elbows pulled inward rear circles
Dark around the eye
Vision blurred
Doctor enters
Resident undisturbed
Hazy and unheard
By virtue of insanity

Streets climb with sewers and madmen
Striking the mind
Teeming with kingly sized rats
Chasing till alley's end
As they scratch
No escape can be had
They lacerate psyche
To shreds of cheese
Gnawing

He rocks to and fro
From voids below
Hell only absurdity knows
White walls melt into cloud colored coats
Of nameless doctors whose stethoscope
Can never hear the heart pummel
Thump . . . thump
Pitiless slow it crawls
While uncanny beads dread upon the brow

Scavengers claw to petrified alley corners
Trapped by brick, white pads, flat beds, garbage cans,
      shredded clothes, sparkling white coats,
      doctors and rats

Mourning Imagination

A plastic body the only requisite for title
From necessity of simplicity this magical world evolved

Until the lonely patch of dirt became a bustling courtyard
Surrounded by puddles from spring showers filled into a gorge
      around a tree that grew into a castle
      and every leaf that caught the sun formed stained glass windows

From soft rags, I built a bed
From a branch, I built a table
An old shoebox, I erected as the alter
      where the queen would pray for better days

Escaping through the opulence of my tiny kingdom
Away from tyrannical punishments
      thrashings that shatter all innocence
      always surrender to imagination

Haven of safety
A diminishing sanctuary
Molded each day to embrace reality a little more
      until nothing remained

By the summer of ten
The tree sprouted only leaves
The shoebox gathered dust in some wardrobe
      and the soft rags tossed aside long ago

The young plastic queen becomes the flesh of a woman
Intelligent
Realistic
Yet mournful

Irish Warriors

Long ago were men that fought for freedom
Still today they debate their right over drink of man
Foam sipped over battles of so many years
Prided heritage of waging war for lands

They knifed down many a great warrior
Landscape surrounding was green without defeat
A green that enlivened the soul
And wrapped the grassy knolls about their feet

Mere men that called themselves to pride
Lined with battlements of marching plaids on lads unripe
On fight they!
As lands stretched rolling vast beneath them
Dying where they stood

But is always true
Irishmen with brew in hand may make them merry
Toe-tapping jigs of lightning speeds
Flutes and fiddlers with bursting bagpipes
In old castle walls of stones and sconces bright
Be the Irishmen that rose at dawn
To fight with freedom in their sight

Walking Staff

This man that needs a dime with walking staff in hand
No less important than our need
Toss off and ignore deprivation in the street
When a simple coin the only wish or plea

For one born with a silver spoon
                may wish for affection never received
Or those in search of vocation
                so status is perceived

Old man needs slippers of twenty years
                or he can't kick back to comfort
The banjo player needs ears to hear
                or silenced without listeners

Maybe a child needs a backpack
                so his school wares will not spill
Or the Scotsman needs a Collie
                or sheep shall roam the hills

Well the man on the corner needs a coin
Who are we to disdain his dime need
Pretend as though he does not lay there
For filth and pestilence no time to spare

As we look away and pass him by
                we hear his call
Only needed is your notice to toss a coin
                is all

That he matters just a moment
                worthy of human eyes
Transforms his staff into a serpent
                suddenly filled with life

Subway Train
The Shoes of Passing People

One shoelace lingers undone, simply sagging to the floor
While the other seems to bounce around
Clumsy young girl with slovenly hair stares longingly

Next is feminine fulsome shoe encircled curtly round the other
Never again to move with the carefree canters of a child
Long gone are those years for businesswoman of longest day

Then come burly unpolished clunkers
Fumbling and squirming to find a seat
Endeavor to climb corporately when the top impossible to reach

Then were high-top black leather shoes
Laced long with thick wide heels for wearing use
Old lady of many children past prays to rest her feet at last

Shining golden shimmering shoes, pumps that perceive the stars
Sit snugly hugged to smooth skinned beauty
Awakens in the night as darkness helps to make her keep

So many shoes characterize these speeding metal monotonous walls
Within them come the walks of life of many
Heading home in search of comfort
Found only by shoes of few

Once the Tempest Doth Run Out

As I sit on the train speeding
Cement flies by me fast
Like the world leaving me behind always
Many call me slovenly
And slovenly I may be
Least I have a home to rest my head and feet

Christmas scents upon the air
As I walk to his city store
Firewood left remains
Splintered in the sky from 'Hallows Eve

A time that I revel
Since witches call me out to create my own kettles
No one knows the secret that I worship hot brews
And hold retched ancient medals of old vendettas
Leaves are brown and crutch upon the streets

I remember autumn leaves coloring skies into auburn wreaths
On every day the 30th of many 'Hallows Eve
A photo I hold tight to pockets
That I carry everywhere
Black and white of mother as I return home
Her death lingers

I hear the howling night dogs not far off
I run the last few dirt stretches
Smell them fowl growling near

Then round the corner comes the homeless man
Thrust a quarter quick upon his hand
Satisfied, he carries on

Through the door swift but safe
Now the regular yelling jags of daily life awaits
After lengthy punishments, I dash to my room
Whereupon I put my music on to wash away all gloom
As Beethoven quiets my rushing frenzy to a lull
My life made to specks compared to his impending doom

I only witchcraft to dabble
Not my heart true
Just mourning the loss of kingdoms in my youth
Those kingdoms I created

Where Irish warriors would fight for lands green and everlast
And slaves would usher rocks up vertical pinnacles
In honor of my Paroahship, lands stretching evervast
Sands waning now

Sliding through my fingers as the tempest doth run out
The tempest of my imagination
Lonely and deprived of friends or even foes
I reside in quiet chambers above my father's store
Above the moors

Happiness I try to clutch
As only a lonely slovenly girl must
And hopeful when I grow, I'll have riches beyond the bust
And when I lay deep in grave
Knowing I shall not be saved
Perhaps I'll grump and gollop
When someone tries to trollop
And prance and dance upon my grave

For what right have they
Not my hard life led
With a father in the country store who calls for me no more
Only to run from dogs that growl vehemently as pests
Eating the rats in alleys

And I a rat myself
Lonely, cantankerous, raucous, beheaded heart

I will struggle for my riches and wear them all in death
Residing heavily around the bones of retched neck
Upon my chest
As I try to rest
Peacefully
Once the tempest doth run out

PART IV

INJUSTICES

Never You'll Know

The fresh upon the table scorned
Lemons in green bowls
Where rests the newest nation

The happiest culture
The porno
The gun child
The teen-like vulture

We did not see
The outcast, unwanted and teased
By the purest of cults
The student groups
Some athletes alike

The perfect looking
The none want for strife
The airy heads all communed round the pool
The inept, the popular, the meaningless group

If inclusion not the request
Amongst all the best
Then surely outcast
With the worst and the rest

Till the tormented brings the guns of these
From a father's cabinet
Upon schoolyard plates
Wherein hiding low
Until the first blow

Strikes the cafeteria to chaos
A phobic squeeze through the yellow hall
Vital juice spills
Eminent falls

As kindred adults may have grown from the foe
Life gone
And never you'll know

Discrimination

The golfer's grass is green
And takes to lawn for presentation
Angry she is at the neighbor who lets weeds surge to life
Uncomely look it has next to her fresh glades
So she snubs her face up at the man with weeds

Many Hours

Occasional bright lit dawn
Brings loss at light for memory of darkest room
Where I sat for many hours encaged in ghastly gloom

Was punished unjust
As I stare beyond drapes to light
Inside a wretched cage
Not much larger than myself
Or filthy roach pawing
And fingerprints of cellmates climbing

Uniformed men mocking the pale flesh
And how they locked me still
When detainment all for naught
Oh, the laughter haunts me still
In gleams of old sunny sill

Forget it I cannot
Those bastards I could not break!
Soon to loose all faculties
For lack of air and shards of bars
Breathing uneven
A hollowed frenzied pace

Heaving chest to blows of breath
Forced inhalation
Reeking vile piles
Urine stench
Helpless and enraged
Inside contemptible cage

As sun reaches darkest corners of the room
Face is masked by memory of their sin to me
Warmth of sun at dawn forever lost to me
The heat across my skin since mask of sin is memory
And all the light that shines from brilliant dawns
Will never penetrate the small dark room
Where I sat for many hours encaged in ghastly gloom

Youthful Life

Oh, dark shadows that crevice the eye
Of this life you have forsaken
What has become of the world
When but a youthful life is taken

Wail I will not do
Shame to give into you
With claws of death you grasp
First what should go last

Funeral home offers no comfort
Voluminous emptiness
Big-boxed room
Dead center
As though a coffin inside a coffin
Unmerciful salon
Empty vault
Where grief construed and taught

Of this life you have forsaken
What has become of the world
When but a youthful life is taken

See our sadness while it lasts
For death is moment short
And relatives soon to leave
Your empty mournful court

Alas, for now we are in your hands
So with us have your way
For when we leave your airless room
Your presence cast away

Oh, dark shadows that crevice the eye
Shame to give into you
So wail I will not do

Cast away without regard
Tossed aside as adolescent slips
From your aged grip
As your menacing cloak is ripped
To expose the skeletal
That quickly melts to sands strewn
Soul ripped from skinless hand
From land and man

When but a youthful life was taken
With claws of death you grasped
First what should go last

Death suspension ends
When lungs exhale their last
Ended is your grasp
First what should go last
Lasts on

Before

To commemorate the cemetery of centuries
Decorated with stone slabs that speak the summary of life
Family and flowers round tombstone's edge

We mourn the loss of this passing

Yet within the mother unborn it waits
To partake that which we already have
Hopeful
It awaits life

Injustice Grand Scale

Encaged in bars behind
Coffins lids tight down
To earth
Grass beaded brightly with morning dew
That funeral day
Thinking of jail times
Sunlight and sills

Reminded of home grasses
Tended for hours upon spring seasons
And fertilized the green to everglade shades
Perfect turf to rest upon
Crossing legs
Counting clouds
Shapes from whites

Neighbor will not tend the terrain
Leaving blades to wild weed and brown
While car shines immaculate clean
Ground left to dither and crunch
Brown from sun singed
Bushes in disarray
Ruining the presentation
Oh, blast!
Why did ghettos past
Settle down beside her fast

Separate the parcels
Count the fresh glades only
Please not the undesirable
Property value sinks below the lead
Grass wielding weeds

Remember jailhouse where many neighbors like
Were kept in
She did not belong in
City cops prodded
Pleased they caught a white
Bombarded and teased
Ghettos, she became part of the roaches
That climbed upon her fingerprints
Walls and bars
Unfair trapping

One scant night as cellblock mate
But none as unjust
When most dastardly acts
Performed toward the small.
       Unknown
       Nameless
       Innocent
The pregnant mother
Not yet showing full belly
Now stands aside this grave
Sorrow for this life lost
But no pity for inward lilies
That burst and bloom each day
Like flowers beside the grave

No consideration for
       Not even grown
Stupidity over neighbors land
Or jailed unjust
Far more grievous crimes here
Soon near

Taking leave from mournful court
As clinicians will her organs sort
Thrust wide
       Till the lily grown inside
       Is tossed aside

Think of grasses longer
Remember jail time more
Honor the empty corpse
All of these seem to soar
> Above little life cast away
> Upon the floor
> Through trash doors
> That never had the chance of youth or jail
> To grow greens and disagree
> Cultivate or discriminate
> All was taken before it was ever had
Sin of injustice grand scale!
Life before the belly in full bloom
Always yearning to partake our earthly rooms
Only to find they hold human minds
Of tyrannical hands that seek its doom

PART V

LAND AND LEADERSHIP

Long Last This Lass the Ruler

Jonquils sell in copious amounts unfettered
        from the harbor vendor
Marched in from seas and woods, on foot, barges and hooves
The Titans have come from so far
Hinterlands
Netherlands
Myriads of men

As though Neanderthals to fare
        the plush plume of unwed gentlewoman
Young to rule the nobles
Sits unerringly aloft the majesty
The ruler and giver of the run
        and the way of savvy

She holds the jonquil steady as the Titans thunder in
        to do her bidding and their best wherein
She may give it as her leisure or keep the shields for sake
Not for what the man has said will her decision make

He kneels in awe of them in front of a gown
Her eye gently wisely looks upon and down
        and sends them on the errand
        and then more men to floors
        and errands and wars thus

Until the room is empty
        and she is left alone
Yet admired
As others inspired
By her stature and her breed
The shelves
Contracted lands and deeds

Under the arm of this young wise maiden,
>"Take this message to the captain.
>>We depart without delay at sunset.
>>Prepare the harbor and the Titans
>>for war."

Yellowstone

Cliff walls echo from yellow stones
Circling eagles play swirling full wingspan
Above the great fault

Earth shakes timbers to fit itself anew
Always breaking into vast ravines delving deeper beneath
Crusts shelved upon layers to plates
Shifting and swelling with speeds cracking
Violent shocking temblors
Upon its floors

Moved till injury
And some to death
By unmerciful reshaping
For new cloaks and smarter shores
So growth may surge greener
Earth's turbulent nurturing of itself
Into continuous cycles

Creating endless lines of faults upon its form
Summoning the eagles to play on and then no more
But again they soar, unaffected by the distorting wrath
As it moves to fit itself, a more comfortable stance
And grooves where water flows, new shores
Left with imposing stones, majestic forms

Yellow stones
Wide thrown
Sit still now
For admiration
Circling eagles
Once again at full span play
From newly composed colors and lands
Hear the echoes

Well-Decorated General

Deploy to the left and the right
        upon associate's request
Certain twain tongues measure humanity on a scale acceptable
Yet undeniably therein lacks within the requestors
Materials of discourse to stimulate
And turn their shifty world to right
        through mechanism of word

Hail to bringers and dawn seekers
Stretch fingers without arthritic grasp
And grab what can be yours
Instead of seeking nifty ideas and sojourn journals
Record victories in archives
And wrap your arms tightly round them
For these are the fortitudes of insides turned out

Seek the embalmer upon your prayers of seedy ways unusual
And latch onto the disembowler of your soul
For only when they gut
Are displays so inhumane without shame
That you can march on this sphere righted upon your name
And proclaim
        that thee are
Mightier than the writer
Expansive beyond the explorer
Humble to all humilities
        and vast thereon
Take this dismembered speech and wear it as a cloak
        of future years
That shall garnish your uniform proud

Great warrior of waving flags
Somehow combined with the mad and the straight
To yield your most precious jewel

Laying your passions on grounds of the dead
      that defended your nation
And declare
      for once
That thee are honorable and humble
And if ever you are unable
Advocate hands shall reach out
And transform you
Into greatest living man
      as they reach their hands
      as only you can command
Medals to your uniform
Decorated and venerated upon this land

Column

Here stands colossal column
Rise in marvel of moony flat up to tip
Scraping skies blue and black
No internal spikes fasten structure to its place
Of pinnacle memorial
The spade in a deck of freedom states
Dealing down to cherry blossoms blooming at the base

Senator men signing signatures
Declaration beyond the Old World
Citizens of such contrasting brilliance
Martin Luther's proclamation to come
All colors converging steadily on the memorial
Love thy neighbor
Emblazoned commandments upon the stone
Infinite hues
Beckoning the column to symmetry

Monument stretches onward mounting with our search for meaning
Soaring on the pinnacle of democracy wrought by thundering placement of the base
Then upward as a plunging sword stabbing the earth into the heavens

Leadership

Cajoling the farmer's field to plentiful
Briskly sweeping to cool the sun
      till growth full of corn
I grace the world atmospheres
Over faces of pain and exultation

As the world sometimes spins opposite my speed
Turning of the globe perplexing the course
Similar to all life that graze their steps
      walking a few years
      then leaping off to leave the world limp
Awaiting the arrival of a new deity to guide them
When another may lead it

I am simply the wind
      that dispels upon leader's on freshest days
Even tyrannies are peaceful in my bellowing embrace
Through cigar filled negotiating rooms
      easily I sift
Proceeding to better atmospheric days that support my blow
Cannot leaders of realms beget the same idea below
For how many fresh winded days must they have

Although I've been known to turn your towns into a tempest
      I urge you to my calmer days
When the horse gallops freely from the post
As the brazen bird chirps uninterrupted by a fury
And the eagle feeds the bear a fish
      when all is hand in hand
Cease superpowers so discontent over continents

Listen
The wind

Perilous Vault

Winds gale past
Furious and fast
      then complacent moaning
As leaders assemble
Emperors, kings and queens
And a spectral form
Confer the plans
Draw drafts upon drafts
Till eminent victory at hand

And all the while
Woman's sack filling with jonquils
Simply bent over yellows picking

Suddenly!
Slated by the ambush
The unexpected
Smattering of life upon the land
Bleeds upon boulders
Yellow scatters everywhere
      from petals to stones

Near around the crevice deep
Man spills upon its sweetness wheat
Where woman picking her wares for sale
Much as the meager life
Has lost her sack
Into wild winds blowing the burly men
Lad of twelve lies beside her feet

Thrashing compounds
Numbers outnumbered
Goliaths lacerate landscape into reds and yellows

Abruptly
A man meets her gaze
From another time
A far off place
Unrecognizable stiff uniform
Deep green with many medallions garnished
Piercing eyes staring down
Bald eagle illuminates his chest

Where is he from
        as the men hissing by lighting fires
        hearing gut wrenching sobs at the weapons splitting
        seconds stretch
Captured by his glare
        from where

Fated future wars
American soldiers plundering peaceful Indianheads
To infantry staving off the British at the run
And the Civil man against himself for colors
        and so on
To the one and two Wars
Great bomb did plummet
        from a new world to rogue nations
Uninterested in global policeman
Still with bombardments on foreign soil

A Pentagon
Blueprints upon drafts
        for frames of battle
Near a spade of supposed free men
Pink blossoms convoluting the base
Fragrance of a whole realm without oppression
        except for that ghetto she sees in his eyes

He continues to stare
Eyes never falling
As the movie plays out lit

The earth shakes violently
Even superpowers cannot control
Splitting land asunder
Frequent shifts
Roar under her foot
The tumultuous rumpus!

Wounds and cadavers enumerate
            around her fractured ankles
As his eyes grow
            human pestilence into a minor foe
With millions gutted for the banner bed
A balding eagle soars above her head
Cawing

Jonquils still flying mid-ear
            landing on belts of bodies
Whose souls transcend
And tell the story
Of hoary repeated days
            wars to come

Abruptly
The victors vanish
Thundering grounds quiet without pummel
Silence strikes impending air to emptiness
Fog sneaks round and up the field as walls
Into a cloudy vector
Surrounding an airless crypt or vault
In which
Blades strewn upon rocks
Half silver
Half red
            so many dead
            so many colors lifeless
Only motion that remains
            oozing crimson
            cawing eagle
            pink and yellow petals
And somewhere far off
            a glimpse of a stiff green uniform

93

PART VI

TALES AND SHORT STORIES

Haunted Forest

Peer out the eerie valley
  the dark road
  the thorn imbedded river
  and past pricklers

Something striking about this forest
Unusual gaudy thick air
Blackest night spilling everywhere
Once through
The path creeps up around
As though a Living Will
Renders the walker useless

How far till the lilies
  where I'll cast away old dorms
  and troubled era
  passes into forms

But for now, in front of me it swells
How far, I cannot tell
If I could turn back
But seems as though I'm trapped
Immersed in ghost-like trees
Night dogs sneaking
Red eyes only and then gone

Oh, how far till my past is away
  and my heart not burdened
  no longer a slave
  to the haunting

Big Foot Bearing Fruit

A crackle
Then a crunch
On broken twigs fallen from mammoth trees
Where walks the boldest of big-bodied foots

Cast a boulder cross the forest floor
Thunder resounded from thrashed rock
But not as loud as the stomping of great beast

Too scared to peer from behind the boulder
Employed as pitiful protection
To scurry or breathe too loud could be your death
For you know
Without staring the grizzly beast in the face
It is the famous folklore of Big Foot
The only one of peculiar race

Rancid heart beats wild
Anticipated sure quick death
As he rounds the redwood close
Suddenly the crunching stops

Silence surrounds the deep woods
Holding breath till shades of blue
Bountiful foot passes in front of you

As though too tall to see you there
Like an insignificant slithering snail
Edging from beneath
Fervent to escape
The largest beast
Of stony awkward gape
Sniffs the air for foretell prey
Beads of water distend upon your face
His steps continue past

As the menacing form traverses woods until dissolution
You notice a tasty fruit dropped beside your feet
Days in wilderness soon to starve
So you famine for a feast

Is great beast merciful

Biting into the tempting juice
Sweet and somehow so dry
Walking from whence you came

Suddenly choking your body quakes
Without warning falling to the forest floor
That is your fate

So it seems this looming savage
Wandering lengthy lands
Does not chew and tear your limbs into a bloody feast
Rather leaves a deathly fruit
There beside your feet

Halls of My Home

Storybook stairwell whispers legends and fairytales
Winding up to landings bordered with brass kingdoms
Ingratiated with mezzanine singers
Choir voices roll and seminole the quartet to whistle

Rotund roof pitched center upward
Etched with cupids of artful dramas
Swinging cherubs thus pictured 'pon the ceiling
From willow mosaics as stars twinkling
Flashing in the geodesic night sky

Ocean waves that sustain ships in oils above
Swell in volumes under highest rotunda yet
To hold erect the seafaring hull in the zenith dome
Solidly held afloat by waves and domes

Beneath rests crown molding from corners to edges
Studded with much layering upon its molded cast
Thickness outward as though to spill
From afar each crevice and overlay admired

Down again unto wall medallions under every arch
Carefully encased shields reveal Tudor's crest upon the face
Encrusted in bronze layers of benevolent leaves
Greenery overlaps in cycles of botany and vines

Down to more arches upheld by gypsum columns
Highly erected loftily amongst the mezzanines
Three levels of framed balconies no less
Fitting crown jewel entry to old opera house

Every arch, medallion, molding and mezzanine aglow
Candelabras of such magnitude melt orange gold
Slightly softening harsh edges of sculpted walls
Romantic reflection of structure upon itself, upon its halls

Domed angels and art forms dance in soft lights leaping
Sonnets harmonize till full pitch climaxing sound
Seemingly integrating edifice with oration

Crowds dissipate
Choir quiets to soothing dull hums
Candelabras dim gilded gold
Secretly old opera house becomes my home

> In a jade-encrusted gown
> I glide perfectly down
> Fashionably late
> Royal subjects await

> As a fair enchantress center stage
> Admiring welcoming crowd
> Come feast with me forever
> For these riches shall not run out

> Dining with kings and queens enthroned
> Waltzing the prince and I betrothed
> Spilling red wines in chalices atop my feast
> Table embellished with every living beast

Grabbed from behind
Lights cruelly brighten
Crowds prod once again in careless canter
Gowns and suits pass swift
Choir penetrates eardrums to uncomfortable clangs
Loud and piercing
Stabbing shame awake
Gothic doors slam fast upon my face

Snowflakes pelt chapped hands once again
In place of cupids singing and dancing up high
Comes realities' dome of empty nighttime skies

Halls of My Home [New Stanza]

No guests await me for dining this day
No dancing, no prince, no feast to display
With torn gloves and cold feet
No gown of my own
Wandering endlessly through empty halls of my home

Basement Shroud

Page me to the outdoors
Where walks life of the norm
Out from under the basement gloom
Enfolded room around its office
Around my form

I type feverishly
Addictively
As daily sun becomes the moon
While I am unaware
Oblivious to worldly tidings

The second I am called out
To greet the sun midday
Instances rush around me

The soggy russet grass remnants of winter
Edged with green sod seedlings
Begging for the spring season
Perennials protrude from the ground into newborn green
Emeralds against tainted remains of winter garden untamed
Bulbs beginning to sprout
The day I came out

A fellow passes limping
Hulking awkward man with childlike, "Hello."
Smiling prettily
Disarmingly

Looking past him to neighboring homes
That have stood in the court a century
Adorning character only historic homes provide
Sturdy beyond the decades
Still standing when I am gone

Young magnolia centers front in yard
Packing with perfect green leaves sprouting richest luster
Thickest durable foliage
Soon white blooms attack the ends wholly
Dispersing fragrances around my stoop

White railings
Picket fences
Slabs of vegetable gardens in the make
Tiny buddings en masse
The early spring quake

Scurry back hitherto
Writings in the basement shroud
Eternal wish of mine to place this desk safely out
So I could punch and pound perceptibly
Under bright noon hours till sun sets purpling
Typing gracefully words unwavering melodies

Outside loathsome basement
Free of the frame
To compose under white shaping clouds
Pleased and proud
Instead of looming in my basement shroud

Question the Lunar Walk

Check the winds that blow the flag
In an airless realm
Where shadows of rocks and astronauts
Varying directions scattered

The race of a Russian dog and American monkey
To orbit with nuclear misgivings
Propelling combative space
For assurance of the victor

A movie with Apollo characters
Documentary
Or fantastical fiction
Indecision

Quandary question from far off lunar
Crater blast absent
Spacesuit no rival for radiation
Melting innards around
The non-lunar town
The Nevada sun
The Vegas night
Where the flag in airy plight

Set tight in desert sands
From conspirator's hands

The possibility

The Alabaster Plant

The awed envied largest terrors crashing trees to twigs
Major mountains into meek embankments
Lakes into drinking ponds
Wherein apparent gargantuan tree sat soaking
Was this tree without bark and leaves

Sudden movement
Entire upper half momentum to shift the head
Now the eyes blinking
My heavens and gods above!
What is this torrent thing
This hulking chewing tops of redwoods
These thumping pounding earth-shaking steps
Oh, what a thing is this

Strikingly, as a mountain in front of a mountain
Where are the normal sizes
Were they eaten whole
Not by this green eater
Then perhaps the fanged one on its back
A searing roar, a deafening squeal
A tear, a venomous brain-splitting howl
Headaches thrown to edges by the shrill
To crack a tiny human skull
The sounds of fury or Hell
Surely Hades stepped up upon the earth today
Taking all empyrean goods away

Smaller terrors and claws upright running
What madness is this
The half-pint venom
The fast perilous hunter in lightning velocities
More privy than the larger
Leaping several to the great back and then like vultures
Muscles from spines and blood spilling
Again the tearing and feasting

Where is he
Most surely final days
And Memnoch on the planet

Step back foolhardy and stop the observance
Search for the fur covered primate man
Find his sanctuary and use it
Sit like him on haunches bruised
Not born yet
Oh, where the cave
Running through the vaporous trees
Vines grow as snakes up logs
Up trees as columns of jade giants

Amid my run
Lifted from the soil
Startled with paralyzing fears as a bloody sweat
Talons gashed inside my spine scorching
Wingspan of a vampire overgrown
Swooped up hard
No mercy
The muscled giant jetlines shores
So high above

Higher yet
The advancing looming space stone
Free-flying rapidly
Somewhere in the distance
Over hills and into the sea plunged
Deep
A blast
A thunderous atmosphere
A red charred sphere
An orange sky
Clouds spitting fire
The ocean sucked away beneath our flying
Before the nest
Then backward detonation of the ocean at once
Forward and out

Out of the crystalline, sheer, shiny and tiny
Beds of glowing cold brilliant from the sun
Hidden slightly beneath the misty winds
Blowing breezes stacked with powders howling
Honing the sun to a dull hazy shine
Glistening into ice dust pelting on the backs
Of figures far away
Forward procession
Striding against the stinging
Bearing the sleet
As though a regular day
The ancient dawns

Animal skins pelt from their backs
Barely seen in far off gusts of a storm turned sullen
Apathetic from the fallen mammoth
To nourish and wear it
On forms dissolving in the white dust
How far
How far has the world bridged in frigid
An endless flat
A twice-paid forbidden token

Now they emerge again
Still pushing onward
Following the mammoth to the new site
Vaguely baby waddles near a grown figure
Hands swathed in fur holding the young through stages
Life immanent depends
Suspends
Above the cool plains of a million miles
Earth is though a circle of cloud
Never blue
Just dark and bright
In swirling white

I call out to them a sapien speech unheard
Amongst the years of nowhere growing fast and near the Bering

So few availed earth of largest bridges
That crack and melt into a small green thing
Here or there till more waters flow
From springs not before seen
I dive and drown

Sputtering
Awakened in the dark to a hissing - a jeering
A twinge of locust-like sounds and a starless night
A step of normal proportion passes
Crunching unnoticing
Not the ferret hunter
A someone
Human-like figure
Slightly crouched - a grunt
The cold so completely gone
Heat and moisture thicken on the skin

A smelly stench
A wonder
A more upright stance
A smaller skull
A hint of smoother hand
And teeth less rummaged without hides chewed

When the option grows

And the finite greens become sprawling jungles
A hidden man we followed the caves
Cavernous swallows wholly mightily
Unlike the mere foragers on ice flats
These were pounding stones into tools
Primitive genius bowls and utensils
Flying spears from knives sharply stricken
Piercing comparable tame creatures

Itching into hives
Insects ravage my limbs
They sit peacefully unbothered

Oh, questionable time
What to do
Shall I be slain here this night

A stick in the sand
A drawing of incipience
Cast beneath my eyes
Incomprehensible vestige
Reflected flames leaping in dark on dirt
Many of them crouched - squatting and staring
Hairy and waiting
Noses so eminent
An ape-like man
All seem as masculine Goliaths
Red-eyed a bit
Staring as fast shifty marbles into my own
Even breasts protruding look alike
Gaping
Disgruntled
Restless
Frozen am I
On the spot of a primordial time

A sudden disinterest or distaste
Turn of ape-like forms away
Stand till nearly full erect
Stubby protruding skulls shift left to right
Picking their wares into a baggage tight
Quick upon the backs
And wrapped
Young one crying to the breast
Move away
The clan and the rest
Moving band to move on
A roaming bunch
Now gone

And so the many centuries unrecorded
Hunters gathered and wandered
Women rotund bellies

Ages of races born
From the ravages of male vulgarities
Never a loving grace
Nor a soft touch
A home-like comfort
Or a miniscule affection
Except mothers for the young
The free land walkers
The mostly warless tribes
The freshest air

I hung there for some hundreds years
Quietly resting in the oblivion
On an alabaster plant

Rooted so deep to cores
A hot lava surging
Continually firing and splitting
The reshaping
Plates divide continents by waters
Into a perfect form
Fitting for the normal steppers
The average fleshed
And fur bearers
The smaller skulls tamed
Into a variance of intelligible forms
From vocal chords
Grew the Aboriginal chants
The fully upright walkers
Into dance
The cosmos observed
Into the ritual, the right, the religion
Sitting on rocks in peaceful wonder
Forever the look into the sky
A curious eye
The search for meaning
Pushing the hunter into a leader
One decision maker
Followers by dozens
Voices convert to vernacular

Despondent dialect
But continual effort grew the barriers from the brain
Into a speech
An understood thing
Off my plant and into clans
From the Dark
Relating into Medieval ideologies

The fully erect
Homo sapient arms spent on the work
The meaningful chores
The somehow farmed and cultured
Into small gardens
Where watermelons and countless pumpkins
Seedlings
The children spit and laugh

Fur hides into woven smooth flowing and sheen
Adorn the human
The ever luckier and creative
Adobe walls and hay pitched roofs
A hearth
A humble way
A familial epicenter
Villages of abodes
Neighbors laugh
Proudly displaying black teeth
Picking them with twigs to clean
Still the odors of life swagger in and out
Through huts, off clothes from perspiration
To the good scents of a hearth cooking
Just the right pot and steam
The looming effervescence of meat and potatoes
Short bliss

When far up the hill a monastery
Leaders of the village
Monks of ridiculous balding centers
And hands held together in endless silences
Squandering the day

III

Not for work
But for prayer
That serves their means
And fits their bill
From chanting rituals and cosmos lovers
Spread the meanings into a god creator
A maker of all born and dead
A turbulent giver
An awesome unknown spectral form
Sitting on a cloud
Watching every detail of the plunder and rape
Pillage village to village
Until the rare found Potato
Spreads Famine
While rats and fleas bite the flesh
Into a vast Plague

From the ground to horses' backs
The warriors did perfect
Their winning chance
Upon perfect blades cut into swords
Shining their own reflections in the metal
Finding their own reflections in the water-top
The ugly, the beauties and the barren
The weak, and the leper's fallen skin
To the highest nobles ruling bits of land
Waging a new collection
Taxation from the creation of a coin
Into church coffers and the noble's pouch
The only forgiveness found in offerings
Tithes to beat the poor man into rags
And more filth than ever before

Thus the early waging wars
From one village over another
Small bands taking lands
Until acreage was dominated by one sect
Sects spanned to millions men
And then the savages
The bloody wars

All for want of domination
The common denominator
Across continents
The now would be Europe
The Russia grand
The Islamic desert
The African wilds
The English proper
And vast thereon
Into kings and chiefs
Ruling alongside healers
Medicine men
The hierarchy of religions ruled by men
To constant keep the flat world in ownership
As though gypsum cast molded to will

Possessions not granted but taken
Like centuries of mutilations
Stripped as it were of all dignity
Rationing the lands to the strongest hands
Ignore needy hands
The weak ever sicker
Till millions die unabashed
Unceremoniously
As opposed to a king or chief
Whose sepulcher made mightier than most lavish homes
The tombs of thrones
Vaulted with an airless death that only surrounds royalty
A silence for his penance lacking
Too late for him
Untimely death to us all

Then amongst the toiling and seeming madness
The scratching itching backs
Of endless foes forsaken
There was an upheaval of sorts
A scrupulous seemingly deigned man
The greatest controversy of a thousand two
A king of Jew
And of all

An imitation
Or a Son of God
With a lesson in the kind dove's way
That pecked at the rabbi's hand and speared the hearts
The offense not withstood by temple ruling
His crucifixion completed in an hour six
Alongside the five hundred each day
The Roman's whip slashed spikes into joints
On any tree or cross
All over the hills - moaning and crying
The nasty deed
As a beast
The unconscientious Pilate
May be plastered upon his own cross a thousand times
So the tigers might eat him slowly
As the gladiator's eyes were punched out
And their bodies exploited in his games of death
The great Roman Empire is it
From the Great Alexander
To the Caesar

Soon the empty chariot charges by
Horseless

As before
Now a Pharaoh is eating his own arm in a red sea
All that remains is a pyramid's prick
And a camel's snout

One of many stories scrolled in a book
A metaphor here or there
A scribbling of some scripture by men
Convenient the heavens inspired
In writings translated a million times
Over the world for kings
Into halls of a dynasty born
A Vatican kingdom
Of jeweled cathedral forms
From marble to mosaics
To the crafty god and Adam 'pon the ceiling

Domes raised with taxes from meager men
When the king of Jews would just as soon sit on a rock
Or a floor
We built a billion pews for our backsides
Enumerating the silly cushion for our knees

The sit and stand mass
The set speech
Repeated and uncharacterized
Monotonous priests humming and singing some dull Latin terse
Verses repeated so often that the Lamb is lost
And walls of costly cathedrals loose their brilliance
Marble looses luster
And stains with shame
In the adumbrate
The mosaics melt into uncanny sparkling tyrannies
Of religious wars from the political
Contusions of irony in the eastern land
A formulated Koran
Of the Mohammed prophet
Sending the sacred rock to Mecca
On a four cornered blanket for each king
Muslim peace to all thinkers

Did Cane or Able own the Rock
Or merely inherit the bombs
For the land thereon
Of turbulent battles over the sprouting golden bulb
Carnage over the men that preached for peace
All religions to the bank
Spending to build domes of worship
When prophets rather give as fish to feed the masses

Soon for science
A thought to the metaphysical forms
Muslims engineering numerals and philosophies
To the western world
Spiraling enlightenment from a wise tower
And the earth into a sphere
Levied by a queen

The flat is gone
The round is here
Exploration of the sphere

Artists query ceilings and sculptures with a magical wrist
Details finest lines on every inch
Expressions etched as oil on the canvas rough
Flawless realism reflected
Adorning every hall in the great Boot

Into museums decorating our cities
With the build-up of hazards
From stacks industrial in the air
And a heifer's bottom
Plaguing cancers and a gaping ozone

Slowing the earth's conveyer core
Until a freeze hits
As a bomb blowing the greens into a white pitch
An arctic sorcerer
May cast yet a third frigid spell

So we reach to strands
And mess with the oracle ladder
The predictor of traits
The common ninety-nine
One different
All of us like all things
A lady like a spider
A man like a bear
And a bear like a spider
Cycles discovered on the genome
Similarities
As the indian sweeps the ant before she steps

While the majority
Once again waiting to dominate
Every size of life
To wield the genome to our will
Shaping nature into a pleasing marble mold

To cure the cancer
And make the child pretty

Absurd spinning world out of control
Constantly trying to tame the masses to a way
A culture, a belief, a fad
A foreign thing
An abject nature
A flittering fancy, a political man, a leader again
A free realm

So free that morality may be dumped as dung
And love thy neighbor to the trash
Familial structure crumbles
The divorces war in countless homes
The available gun
One young fired
Free press covers the story
Spreading the gun idea
To the rest
Till the schoolyard
A thing of past

Premier buildings built as millions the price
All for a seat in leather high back chairs
Suited with frivolous little ties
All the care for if a share did drop
A Wall Street heart
A lifeless pot

Oh, the frenzy hurts my soul indeed
And I got lost somewhere
On an alabaster plant

That is the last I remember

Before the throng
As soon as I came to speak with clans
When all could speak

As soon as the brain grew from the barrier
When the dance began
And I chanted with them at the fire

When the creativity was exposed
And then the simple Lambs
I can't remember since

Perhaps, it is wiser to forget

And only remember the peace before the intellect
Or the Lambs that offered a dove
Whose beak did pierce my heart

After all
Soon we'll be marching on the ice again
Back to the Bering Strait

Fact or Fiction

From fields into halls
       inside the shroud
I have tainted the day into a field
       of glowing candelabras
By a thorn prickling patch
       bearing fruit
       of a growing haunting
Which sets astray the untimely task of memory
Whose folklore is rich

And I, alone in woods
On an alabaster plant
Does it breathe as it was born
Or did we mold it
Is it gypsum or life
Ice or petal

Shaking the hand of a Sasquatch
That has followed me a world over
With the giant shadow behind me
Now in front to greet me
The final confrontation
       of a query
A controversial swaying
       from far off lunar
We did not walk
Or a victory sure

Like the vague shadow trailing me always
What is reality
Scanning the memories
Pulling them from the shroud
To find fact or fiction
Never to be found

As the opera hung a mezzanine
      in the inappropriate street
And left it to squander
Unfed
From where they sang sonnets
Beautifully
     and afraid
     of the loneliness compounded

Booming as the pit of an orchestra
Vibrating this plant
Into a prince dancing
Around an endless feast

A burden I carry
This Big Foot on my back
Of regrets and proud moments
In a fiction or fact

PART VII

PHILOSOPHY AND TIME

The Republic

The path of a new dominion
Fleeting as a fallen nova
To the depths of Cicero

Under the Board

Select the tendrils
        of only blond or gold
Stricken from the foe
The brown russet
The colorless sunset

Preach against children
Beset in bad ways
        or seem to upset and oft
Uneasy the ways

Ignore
Leave them pleading
        for the soul that sets bleeding
From unwanted traits
        and gaunt-like shapes

Below the child from under the porch
        who sits hiding
Wishing to be as fair as the golden ones
Too far from the effects of beauty
Never informed of deeper possession

So out he sits
Young derelict
Consuming profanity spoken of his visage
Learns that all do detest
The unpretty child under the board
Of the slab of the porch
        hidden away

The Academy

Perpetuating perfection
From every curve and thin line
Tuxedos
Ball gowns
Gaping wide to the breast
Expose your best
Diamonds and rubies borrowed

This eve of the awards

Waiting lines of limousines
Harassing golden statue circling
Looming above the lens
Red carpet
Center aisle
Never touch soles to pavement
Below hair brushed up
Spread out into lavish curls
Some with waves and straight back

A sophisticated look

Clamor over perfection set on all sides
The long rides
Lines long
A mere glimpse of characters known to all
Seizing the streets with blockades
Preventing the crowds
Ardently awaiting the grand descent
Never a moment the camera strays
Unrest amongst the hustling and bustling of the pre-show
Nerves will not suffice

On a classical face

Up the long aisle
Media never ends underfoot
      and pretend
Starved for a month, a year, four or more
      for the lithe-like look of a Hollywood shore

Forbid sweat to pour
      or cosmetics to drip
Perfection the requirement
      of this annual trip
Now come sit
      until the names are called

All for a balding statue

The Vegetarian

Dogs assembled by hunting idiots

Slaughterhouses chemical and cannibalize the cows till methane destructs

Ozone gaping above foot and mouth diseased hoofed things

Eating the heifers till mad disease takes the dumb

Now to elk and deer plagues

Strike the hunting idiots once again

For all the blades and rifles that took them down

Creatures revenge

Soon to die stupidly upon multitudes of vegetation

Routine

Leery to the routine of it all
The hum drum of
Not to discuss just sleep, work or wake
Rather to speak in pretense, then sincerity
And then again the next day

Morning brings the coffee bean to boil once again
Consuming wakefulness to dreary eyes
That would rather back to bed
But must march spiffed in garb of work appropriate
Till day end of evening meal and nightly prayers
To then again slumber
Only to wake afresh ripened for routine of years

No worry when the clock of similar days finally unwinds
And your final breath exuded
When soul creeps from old bones into air
Keep yourself from worry
Do not lament
Do not wail
Weeping for fear of this passage — mere ludicrous!

For when we pass past ourselves in darkness
Light will emerge unbroken like the regular dawn
Death awakens sleep nights to light mornings bright
My friend dear of years
Do not spear fears into ears
But hear right here!
Routine propels beyond the sphere

Wisdom

Deities die out when youth believe they know better
Prosperity surpassing propriety
Plump with the food of easy access
Pompous to sit and coddle ineptitudes
Speaking grand tales to impress or profit awards
For nodding heads of approval

The older one knows better

Merry-Go-Round

Merry go
Merry go
Merry-go-round
The horse of pink strong steed
Showing
Muscles curved up from shaft legs
Wide expanse upon the carousel
Dozens of flying fast steeds
As the child hoorays and folds upon
The horses dazed and pleased

Wherein the candy
Is left without notice more
When upon the steed of healthy stealthy
Imitation horse
Round we round
On merry-go-round

The sound
The sound
Of the song fairgrounds
As the child upon the pink steed
Clasps the golden ring
Laughs and jeers of formative years
Pride to be green
Like lands that stretch so over
And cover plains of youth plentiful
When all is radiant with unripe years
And the mind is soaring through the vessel
Of round and round
And merry-go-round

Background chants
Of adulterous acts
Soon to become

Befall and take grievous weary
To stressful works
And labor long
To hours of strain not yet renowned

Simply not found
In this small spinning town
Child seethes upon the present
With colors spectacular

Spinning adult silent cocoon
Fitting inside to normalcy appear
And duplicate don suits
Worn to prove worthiness
To calculate complicated sums
In reports
Many adulate
Expected deadlines
Somnolent computer puncher
Hands upon keys
Only to climb
Unworthily
And discern that façade brought
Is all that matters to the bringers
In this modern epoch
Of inter-web spinners
And round to more board meetings
Hoping to find
Never time
When a call then
On mobile phone
To again meetings extrapolative
And round and round
Through rooms unadorned with personal effects
Loaded with the professional airless
Rooms upon rooms
That bored and stiffen to inner neglect

Merry-Go-Round [New Stanza]

So free
Child free!
Upon the pink horse
That is your steed
And celebrate upon circles as you spin carefree
Feel the buckle under foot
And pretend you're the Old West
Or ingest the embodiment of any princess
Take kingdoms in your golden rings
Reach on
Through the carousel
Of dreams upon dreams

       Before the spinning ends
       And the ride winds down
       As a quiet compeller
       Of middle-aged compounds

Hold on to the spinning
The epithet waiting
Overlapping upon curls
Round your soft head is shading
And tell all the onlookers
Adults sure they are
That you are the king in carousel arms
And douse those who doubt
That surely you'll bound
Forever and always
Round the merry-go-round

The Gift of Sanguine

Fire bees pass them by easily
Strutting with a bounce
A flit of hand or hair
No cares

Red topless cars speeding
To the stately home in a comely neighborhood
Landscapers lavish the lawn
Perfect green

Her nails not a chip
Flesh not a wrinkle
A tall mature steady gaze
Does not shift
Sure as the bold step in front
Sanguine

Until the many bedrooms unfilled
        and no laughter off the stoic archways
Where equipment or software
        in some type of den or office
        instead of a bed
No place
        for the dust mites framing a fingerprint

Open the present and give a good look
Night tea and scones
Alone with a book

Splinters

Has not the man overworked it
The board nailed to the post as it were

Somewhere in the mailbox rests a charlatan dogma
A degree of higher learning
Whose wood is splintered

Waiting for the sander
Who will not come
Nor will the degree unless the box is opened

Perhaps the splinters make a cut more worthy

We Too Shall Be Forgotten

Castle climbers
Ruin revelers
Roll up your sleeves and move the boulders
Round and up
And down again
To construction sites that line with men

Build the land
Into sprawls of convenient dwelling
Make the store nearer to the home
Make the capitol the closest dome
Beat the stick upon the engine
Till locomotives run in smaller sizes
For everyone

Forget former years
Lament the Lamb - but lose it
Study Joshua and Abraham — ludicrous!
Only see ancient years upon a church
But go on
And build you up
Till highest perched
Scraping skies with metal formed points
So high
So high
Till halls of glass seem to sway
And towers glean the eye

Cover the blocks with cement and software
Meter the streets for coins everywhere
So none is for free
And each second profits
As you elevate to floors
High above the metropolis

Goodbye Bethlehem
Goodbye to the Lamb
Close books of the lyricists
And solidify your land
With machinery and hands
Upon the earth dug out dirt
Gaping wide
With enterprise

Goodbye to philosophers
Goodbye to old thinkers
And toil the soil
Tatter and tinker
And stone upon stone
Goodbye to old thrones
Hail faces upon green paper
And spend without thrift

Till far in the future our Wall(ed) Street(s) a myth

First Lesson on Greed

My old gamblin' dive
When I was five
Prairie of slots
Tuckered and tried

Wheelchair rolls up
I pounce on his lap
Grab hold of the lever
He sets for my grasp
Pennies down the shoot
Praying for bars or fruits
Single or double or triple bars
Cherries blueberries or plums will I land
Flying fast all the colors
Till the raise of my hand
With a click, click, click
My fortune is found
Profusion of pennies roll haplessly down

All the pennies are mine
Soon after implored
Sharing required
To play one more
Lip thrusting a pout
Begrudgingly passing my own coins out

Wheelchair squeaked to a stop
On his lap I did plop
To play again and again
Handles on slots
Fruits over bars and the happily more
To the penny dish falling
Coins for us all

The Glastonbury House

Behold!
Is not this lamb the maker of the wool
Burdened by all errands on the trusty path
A cover to carry you through the night
            and the night does not care

Spun on and around the wheel of a loom
Oft the needle to a subjects arm
Instead of the spinning there
            that could be done

Why now does this man lie on the corner
Glazed eyes as though a Medusa with flopping limbs
Seems the pools of Poseidon float him on his belly
What has happened to the weaver

The maker of warmth and ills retriever
Up the hill inside the Glastonbury House
Wherein the tower he used to wrap our backs
Now the shepard has lost his profit
            and our backs have gained the cold

Misery Unchecked

To the sorrow
And undignified
Without grace
Uncanny teardrop
That falls unchecked

Does stress wrack the bones finery
Into a wrung out thing
A perversion to the soul
The worry compounds
Until the finery is gone

(Untitled)

Please someone suppress the oats of a man unsown
For his freakishness spatters everywhere

Consideration of Clock

What sets our motion to waste or wonder
As simple as the blade or complex as a witness
Clocks scavenging away the moments

Gales usher torrential storms
Of immortal's rods upon the ground
That splits the second into illumination

       as they are not wanton of the time
       or needed therein

Of a moment gone and new arisen
While the rest must quickly siege the earth
With talon strength

The acidic flesh of a wastrel
The death of unwanted spewed
The untold story of a life

       ignored and unheard
       since unclaimed and none endured

Hypocrisy to the soul
Or whatever inner vibe one holds
Each day rationing away the ticking

Not a mountainous wind of a thousand kites could make them fly
Or a heel could make them run
Not an open eye

       to the opportunity

The Bribe

Back away and leave us to our chores
You see as though a simpleton joker
That all revolve around your tokens

When you send the outlandish and banish
As though a lass to weave an unworthy quilt
For your cold posterior

Wear it as a blame of all seasons
As a coat of shame
For sending the young one to that realm

Off with you and horrid bags of tokens
Pay us not what we already own

Insipid Hourglass

Call the insipid out to persuade
Contort
Transform old days away

Sunlight emblaze
Outdoors
Upon your face

Unsullied
Start anew
Awaken cadaver with lightning strikes
Set askew
All regular earth doers

Split the sidewalk in two
Cracking threes and fours
Insert yourself perpetually upon the floors

Sow the seeds spreading gluttonous
And lengthen the mind round eternal reels and vines
For paramount tests
And pass them all with highest grades

Turn your talents out and sear them down
Before the sands of graves
Emanate

Exulted Ends
I Walk to Them

Rays of sun that blind
And scorch the green seed to tree and flowers that bloom
Round my yard
In loud July colors
       then August silently

Except portentous men speaking
To unreasonable minds
Voices rise to hopelessness
Death surely imminent in tones of war
And destruction soon to follow
       not yet known to us

Inside my humble oasis of home
Soon slumberous in dreams
       attempting sleep

Power ends
Alarm clocks set astray to blankness
Moroseness and a frightened breath
The untimely stud of bomb's ends do ingratiate
Through black unprivy to stars
       in our skies

Nuclear shuts out all power made by hand
       away and leaves us
Only on our human head to canter
       as a canteen
Sleep takes ominously to breathe wide open
       again relaxed

Seemingly for the regular night I did lie
Sudden heat waking eyes shifting to hall window
Movement of silo quietly large sneaks by

Floors beneath shift front and back
Sucked up and thrashed
Collapse!
Columns fall out as home sinks beneath
Then quiet
Seedy still in wakefulness

Who forgave me my forsaken

      as though part of a dream
      head burns as singed forests

Did I forgive the trespass

Lifted from feathers forward through waist
As corpus burns quick hot
Then thrusts bones deep into disintegrating bed
Cotton beneath is gone
Lifted from the chest to our annihilation
Thrown back into our exultation
Devastation!

Hello farthest of fathers!
Wreak great greetings to your wrath!
As you pull from brains what is worthy
      if any worth

Soon releasing trees
Pivoting to the lawn of my backyard backwards
And I see someone in the flaming garden
Now calming to regular greens
Those that died wave me to its charm
      and I walk to them

Simultaneous

Round the shoulder and over
Down upon petals that mourn
Now rising in a pink twister to the gray sky
A tulip broke and bent to the wind
Or a breath
From an unknown form
        that I did not breathe

Humidity swept out with chills
And I
To turn a knob
Endless round the door of a century before
So many have turned it
On the porch
A swaying silhouette
        that is not mine

Through the entry
Floorboards termite chewed to dust
Entirely until new floors built upon floors
A step next to mine
And somewhere a perfume
        that I do not wear

Collapsing to the cushion
Of a couch from an antique venue
Many refurbishing fabrics ripped and tossed
And the fillers dumped
Until the numerous sitters
Can only observe the mound of infested white
Wafting to the right
A pipe
        that I do not smoke

Enough trivial visions and scents
Exhaustion must be the contributor
So to a chamber sleep
Before a deeper spell
A rambling talk next to me
          that I did not speak

Dawn brings the tulip again
Digging fine soil into pansies
And yards of more green
Where all the souls that walked here

Amazing how the ground replenishes itself
In time for new feet
Never worn sunken and gone
As the feet themselves
Only to return in a whisper
Bumping into each other
Through Einstein's timeless void

As pink petals continue
Against each other
In spiraling cyclones
Up to gray

Serendipity

(Summary of Parts I - VII)

Observe below
The temperate forms
Under swords
The royalty comes
As trumpeters play
And billions bow their heads
To recognize
Propelling innovators of our times
As yellow jonquils cascade
Upon cut tulips in the air
The celebration begins grand scale

The cathedral wakes and sways

Queens staking
Over men of the run
Heartily upon the swords
Uplift the youthful life
Up to wishful domes
Mobile in kingdoms
Fitting the manta rays on shelves
In a library royal
Of recorded teen deaths
The gunshots
The perilous wars of men
Wherein silos sneak by
As example for the young
That tramples upon the pages
Of history upon the stages
In naughty books
Inside the temple splintered
Enlivened to ensconce the skills of men
Stealthily into busts

Roaming upon the free land
As night dogs
And the European feudal
With a Muslim blanket
Always wrapping life
Into new forms
Borne
Sanguine excavators
Farmers cultivate the storm
All magically dust the soil
Into air scattered everywhere
Upon London roofs
And duck ponds
Falling

The cathedral shakes and reverberates

Now below
The temerarious forms
From red and blue velvets
All the rooms
Upon halls of roots and trees of tall
Reaching to moldings
That crown our forests
Ever scolding
With the haunting Big Foot of peculiar race
The one-eyed Jupiter descends in spades
Rounding foot of forest
Of a thousand wines

The cathedral quakes and chimes

In marches nobles
The adorned
The garnished men
Female rulers arise again

Buckets and brooms surround and distend
The presidents and emperors
Eerily upon our lands
And on the shoulder, one yellow petal
And on the pond, one duck
The murky lands vast and the insane rat
Lonely scampers across the floor
And climbs the walls to those more like
Up columns that ring freedoms blaze
Within the glaze
Upon rooftops sullen
And the operatic voices travel back
To mezzanines
From the ample woman's voice
Over the piano in the din
The rich therein
Bastions tower
Sits the weaver
Sewing all to one goal
Up vertical slanted Pharaohs
Upon sands
That demand
As only the incumbent General can command
The slovenly child from the carousel
To fighting lands
Or to business streets walked
Inward sculptures
The sepulchers
The business culture
Before the epithet shading
Suits donning ties over warriors
Uniforms
In the sorrowless realms
Of Einstein simultaneous
And infinite topless tulips
In the garden of one small flower
Extolling petals
Upon the royalty that now in marches
And all between

From sin unjust
And equivocates
The epic of man dismembered
Or dislodged to streets
The wholly desolate
Sequestered and conjoined again
Upon the realms of times lucidity
Of repeated errors
On the alabaster plant
Of a tribal chant

Cathedral clamors full pitch!

Awake the in and out torrent of humanity
Thrust routine daily
Upon the table scorned
And pound the gavel
Justice prevails the caller of good and evil
For equilibrium

As balance perpetuates
The hunter to the prey
Back to a dragon strung
Plucking to tame our purpose
To intelligible forms
Inside a Good Book

When on the bee the truth is found
Cycling all the past upon the present floor
Within which blossoms future forms
Ideologies abundant thread
Forebear the quilt we all must bed
From unbroken layers
Firmament to land
Connected through a solar strand
Tossed onto the unexpected
Prodigious land
Of a good fortune global
Serendipitous hand